# MRS PEPPERPOT
## AT THE BAZAAR

MRS PEPPERPOT AT THE BAZAAR
A RED FOX BOOK 978 1 782 95352 4

First published in Great Britain by Hutchinson,
an imprint of Random House Children's Publishers UK
A Random House Group Company

Hutchinson edition published 1959
Red Fox edition published 2013
This Red Fox colour reader edition published 2014

3 5 7 9 10 8 6 4 2

Text copyright © Alf Prøysen, 1958
English translation copyright © Hutchinson Children's Books, 1960
Text abridgement copyright © Random House Children's Publishers UK, 2005
Illustrations copyright © Hilda Offen, 2005

Red Fox Books are published by Random House Children's Publishers UK,
61–63 Uxbridge Road, London W5 5SA

www.randomhousechildrens.co.uk
www.randomhouse.co.uk

Addresses for companies within The Random House Group Limited can be found at:
www.randomhouse.co.uk/offices.htm

THE RANDOM HOUSE GROUP Limited Reg. No. 954009

A CIP catalogue record for this book is available from the British Library.

Printed in China

Penguin Random House is committed to a sustainable future for our business, our readers and
our planet. This book is made from Forest Stewardship Council® certified paper.

MIX
Paper from
responsible sources
FSC® C018179
FSC
www.fsc.org

# MRS PEPPERPOT
## AT THE BAZAAR

**ALF PRØYSEN** ❖ **HILDA OFFEN**

RED FOX

One day Mrs Pepperpot was in her kitchen with her young friend Hannah. Hannah was busy scraping out a bowl and licking the spoon, for the old woman had been making gingerbread shapes.

There was a knock at the door and in walked three very smart ladies.

"Good afternoon," said the smart ladies. "We are collecting prizes for the raffle at the school bazaar. Do you have some little thing we could have?"

"Oh, I'd like to help," said Mrs Pepperpot. "Would a plate of gingerbread be any use?"

"Of course," said the smart ladies.

But as they were leaving they laughed behind her back. "What a funny old lady and what a silly prize!"

Mrs Pepperpot was very proud and pleased that she was going to a bazaar.

Hannah was still scraping away at the bowl and licking the sweet mixture from the spoon. "May I come with you?" she asked.

"Of course," said Mrs Pepperpot. "Be here at six o'clock." And she started making another batch of gingerbread shapes.

But when Hannah
came back at six
the old woman was
not there and she
could hear an odd
noise coming from
the table.

The mixing bowl was upside down, so she lifted it carefully. And there underneath sat her friend, who was now as small as a pepperpot.

"What a nuisance!" said Mrs Pepperpot. "I was just cleaning out the bowl when I suddenly started shrinking. Then the bowl turned over on me. Quick! Get the gingerbread out of the oven before it burns!"

But it was too late. The gingerbread
was burned to a cinder.

Mrs Pepperpot sat down and cried, she
was so disappointed.

But suddenly she laughed out loud and said, "Hannah! Put me under the tap and give me a good wash. We're going to the bazaar, you and I!"

"But you can't go like that!" said Hannah.

"Oh yes, I can," said Mrs Pepperpot, "as long as you do what I say."

First she asked
Hannah to fetch a
silk ribbon and tie
it round her so it
looked like a skirt.

Then she told her
to fetch some tinsel
from the Christmas
decorations.

Hannah wound it
round and round to
make a silver bodice.

And lastly she made a bonnet
of gold foil.

"I've promised them a prize for the bazaar and a prize they must have," said Mrs Pepperpot. "So I'm giving them myself. Just put me down in front of them and say you've brought a clockwork doll. Then pretend to wind me up so that people can see how clever I am."

When Hannah got to the bazaar she put the wonderful doll on the table.

Many people clapped their hands and crowded round to see. "What a pretty doll!" they said. "And what a lovely dress!"

"Look at her golden bonnet!"

Mrs Pepperpot stood completely still and Hannah pretended to wind her up.

Everyone was watching. And when Mrs Pepperpot began to walk across the table there was great excitement.

"Look, the doll can walk!"

And when Mrs Pepperpot began to dance they started shouting with delight, "The doll is dancing!"

The three smart ladies sat
in special seats and looked
very grand. One of them had
given six coffee cups for
the raffle, the second a lovely
table mat and the third
a beautiful iced cake.

They thought the doll was wonderful.
Mrs Pepperpot went over to speak to
them. The three smart ladies were very
pleased.

"Come to me!" said the one who had
given the coffee cups.

"Let me hold her a little," said the lady with the table mat.

"Now it's my turn," said the lady with the iced cake. "Well, I must say, this is a much better prize than the one that funny old woman offered us today."

Now she should never have said that. . .

Mrs Pepperpot leaped out of her hand
and landed PLOP! right in the middle
of the beautiful iced cake. Then she
waded straight through it. The cake lady

screamed, but people were shouting with laughter by now.

"Take that doll away!" shrieked the second lady, but *squish, squash* went Mrs Pepperpot's sticky feet, right across her lovely table mat.

"Get that dreadful doll away from us!" cried the third lady.

But it was too late. Mrs Pepperpot was on the tray with the coffee cups, and began to dance a jig. Cups and saucers flew about and broke in little pieces.

What a to-do!

Suddenly it was time for the raffle.

"First prize will be the wonderful clockwork doll," someone said.

When Hannah heard that, she was very frightened. What would happen if somebody won Mrs Pepperpot?

At last the winning number was called – 311.

Hannah looked at the ticket in her hand. What a piece of luck: it was number 311!

"Hurray!" she cried, and showed her ticket.

So Hannah was allowed to take Mrs Pepperpot home.

Next day the old woman was her proper size again.

"You're my very own Mrs Pepperpot," said Hannah, "because I won you at the bazaar."

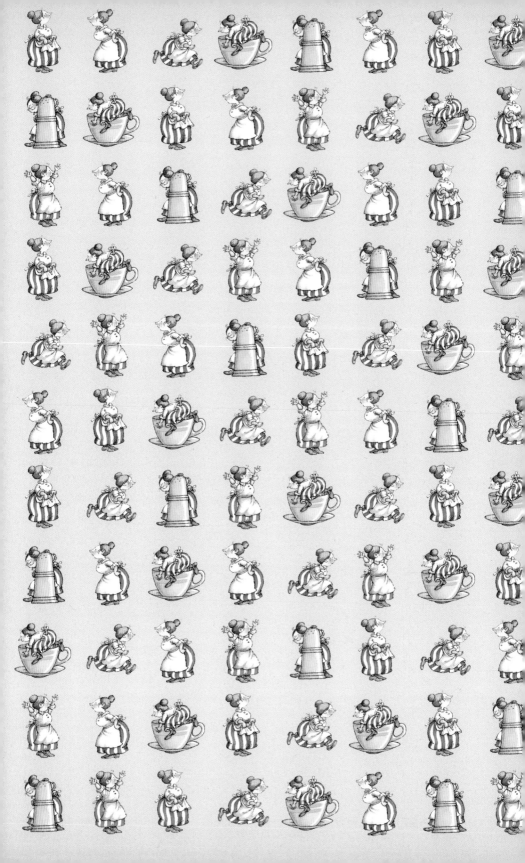